S0-AAA-712

Habits

100-word stories

by Susan Sink

Habits

All rights reserved © 2012 by Susan Marie Sink

No part of this book may be reproduced or transmitted
in any form or by any means, graphic, electronic, or
mechanical, including photocopying, recording, taping,
or by any information storage retrieval system, without
the written permission of the author.

susanmsink@gmail.com
http://susansink.wordpress.com

ISBN: 978-1-300-24195-9

In memory of my grandmother

Alma O'Donnell James

(1912-1991)

Table of Contents

Habits

Some said it was an important part of our witness to the world. Others said it was strange to dress as a fifteenth century German woman in 1960s America. Some said it made people trust us and respect us. Others said it made people self-conscious and guarded. Some said it was putting on airs, pretending to be clergy. They said we needed more solidarity with the laity. Others said the change would lead to sin. In the end, we took off our habits. For weeks, all you could hear was the hum of sewing machines. My first dress was blue.

Home Visit

I managed an extra home visit only because my
mother was ill. My brother Frank arrived for me in
the truck. In the back were fifty chickens in crates.
They squatted in the hot wind and I was full of the
scent of the farm by the time we arrived. I tried to
keep my habit clean. One afternoon I accompanied
Frank to the lake. He fished and I read a book. A
little boy called down from the ridge: "Hello,
Sister!" waving enthusiastically. We didn't know
him. My brother laughed, and I did too, though
really I was proud.

Life's Liturgy

When we children were ready for bed, we said:
"*Gelobt sei Jesus Christus.*" And to our "Praise be
Jesus Christ," the adults responded: "*In ewigkeit,
Amen.*" Going to bed was liturgical. We lived our
faith, practiced its words and gestures. It made
climbing the stairs to bed a procession. Even the
barn was a sacred place. We kept it clean as though
Mary and Joseph could show up at the door any
evening in need of a place to stay. We knelt to tie
our shoes, baked bread with scrubbed hands, lit
candles for the dinner table, said our prayers.

Music

Our oldest brother, Father Innocent, was in charge
of the music department at the university. When
the first Victrolas arrived with piano records, he
invited us over. Every spring when the orchestra
played, our mother would take us by train through
the country towns and we'd walk through the
woods to the abbey. The orchestra filled the hall
with beauty that crushed our hearts. Afterward, we
joined Father Innocent to hear the classical
records. Many years later, I led a choir of our
women and their men. I played the *Salve Regina* on
their grand pipe organ, just that once.

Vice

"I'm told you smoke," the aspirant director said.

"Yes."

"Heavily," she added. "When was your last cigarette?"

"In the car on the way here, with my brother."

After the lecture on morality, she said, "I don't know myself, but the priests tell me it's hard to quit."

When I needed a cigarette three days later, I went to her with the pack.

"I'll have Father Wilmer smoke his evening cigar in my bathroom," Sister Renata said. "You go in afterward; no one will know."

Sitting on her toilet, I smoked four cigarettes, then left the pack.

I never smoked again.

Formation

We entered as adolescents, and the strict regimen motivated us to push the boundaries. The stories are all the same—propping open windows and sneaking out to the movies, or worse, sneaking others *in*. Plenty of Sisters on night watch turned a blind eye to lateness, and other times there were minor punishments: memorizing psalms, kitchen duty, extra hours in choir or *lectio*. We weren't allowed to communicate with the novices, so we found a way to pass notes through our trunks. The notes said nothing. We were girls.

Why did things change? Things had to change. Everyone knew it.

Names

Every one of us took a unique name. There were more than twelve hundred Sisters when I entered, so it seemed every name was taken. You could find novices walking in the cemetery looking for graves of early Sisters whose names weren't in use, or scouring the *Lives of the Saints*. Our director asked me if I liked the name Margaret. "Very much," I told her, "but all the forms are taken." She recommended Margretta, the Irish form. When I visited the Yankton monastery the prioress said, "Margretta! We don't have one of those. I'll have to write it down."

Particular Friendships

One night Hilda, also a novice, had a nightmare
that I had been expelled from the convent.
Without thinking, she climbed into bed with me. It
was that simple—she lay her head on the pillow and
was able to fall right to sleep. She woke up the next
morning terrified of consequences, practically flew
out of the room.

Word got out, and I was reprimanded about
"particular friendships." I said we were not
particular friends but *genuine* friends. A year before
she had slept four girls to a bed on the farm. "She
was homesick," I said. "That's all."

Hitching

Sometimes Fran and I would sign out and write:
"We will be picked up by Aunt Hildegard." We
always hitched to town. One Sunday we wanted to
see a film. The bishop was visiting and stayed late.
We had to sneak out, change clothes and get to the
highway for a ride. Who do you think stopped for
us but the bishop himself! "Are you girls from the
convent school?" he asked. "We were with you all
morning," we answered. "Well, you got an early
start on me." He drove us to the theater and even
paid for our tickets!

Typhoid

Most thought it came in Mrs. Pichetti's tomato
sauce that Gigi shared with us. The Pichetti family
got typhoid and then so did twenty-four aspirants
in our class of thirty-six. They took us to a separate
wing in the hospital, and the rest of the class was
quarantined at the convent. We had such high
fevers our hair and eyebrows fell out and we were
skin and bones. It's a miracle no one died. They
didn't tell our families at first; anyway, we couldn't
have visitors. Later they brought us week-old
newspapers and after we read them they
were burned.

Typhoid 2: Confession

After a month in the hospital, there was a week before summer break. The aspirant director said, "It's time to go to confession."

I was too weak to kneel, so I stood. Father asked, "How long has it been since your last confession?"

"I don't know," I answered.

"What?"

"I have been so sick!"

"Oh, all right then, just say your sins."

"I can't remember those either! I'm sorry, I just don't remember!"

He paused. "I don't think you committed many sins during this time anyway, so I'll absolve you and you will leave in the good grace of God."

Mary

I asked for 'Conrad' or 'Jean.' Sister Lucretia said
to me, "You're getting a pretty name, much nicer
than your sister's." (She got Sister Omer.) I almost
fell over when the prioress pronounced the name
Lawrence. I was ashamed to tell my parents about
it. My mother always said, "Lauren, like Laura." I
went to the novice director and told her I didn't
like it. She said, "Well, just put 'Mary' in front of
it." As a nurse it was easy for the doctors to call for
Sister Lawrence, and I got so used to it I never
changed back.

Crows

"*Caw! Caw! Caw!*" we heard every time we went outside, always walking in groups of two or more. The kids called us crows. And once, downtown, a group of college boys who had been drinking (though it was mid-afternoon) stumbled upon us, surprised, and one said, full of gravity, "Blessed be to God." We laughed, or probably giggled. I think the layers of clothing, or the life, made our laughter soft. All we wanted was to go unnoticed, and, of course, we stood out everywhere. We knew we didn't belong in the world. We laughed louder inside the convent walls.

Turkey Girl

I was sick with whooping cough as a child. I was so puny, Sister said: "You need sunshine and fresh air." So she put me to work with the turkeys. I fetched water in two four-gallon pails. I filled them at the pump, climbed over the fence and brought them to the barns. The work made me very strong. Our incubator held three hundred eggs. Four thousand turkeys we had at our peak, enough to feed us and sell. We loved those birds! We put Vicks vapor rub on their throats when they were sick like they were little children.

Cellarer

We had our own meat, dairy, fruit and vegetables.
We canned produce and processed meats. We had
sixty-gallon crocks of sauerkraut and everything else
in gallon jars. I bought other goods by the rail car;
Del Monte would tell me they had a carload and
we'd split it with the hospital. Every Thursday two
men would go to the cellar and bring bags of
potatoes on a two-wheeled cart. The older Sisters
would come to the porch to peel and cut the eyes
out while they said their rosary. The three bins for
garbage were marked: Pig Scraps, Cans, Bones.

Gym

For gym we wore a uniform: black sateen, very full bloomers, a white middy blouse, black tie, black cotton stockings and white tennis shoes. In the dressing room it was total chaos, stockings and ties flying. In class, Sister took attendance. We answered, "Present, full dress." But let's say you couldn't find your tie, and so you flung a stocking around your neck. Then you answered, "Full dress, stocking hanging out." That was a half absence, to be avoided. We did calisthenics, marching and passing a ball around. Competition was forbidden as unladylike. It wasn't worth getting undressed for, really.

Prevention

Sister Jeanette never excused a student for having a
cold because she believed in prevention. If you kept
your feet warm and dry and your head covered, she
said, you could stay healthy. One morning she
checked a nest of baby owls and the hem of her
habit got wet. She got a terrible cold and couldn't
talk. She still came to class and wrote our lessons
on the board. But we didn't blame her. It was a
once-in-a-lifetime opportunity and she did it for the
sake of education and research! Sometimes one has
to take a risk to learn.

Gifts

One of the patients asked me to write up a letter from his mother. The letter had gotten wet and he just wanted the words. The others wouldn't do it, but I said I would. He gave the pharmacy a much needed L.C. Smith typewriter for typing up prescriptions, which I had been writing by hand. He wanted to give me something personally, so I asked for a plastic apron. Plastic was just coming out then. Anyway, medical records wanted the typewriter. I told them: "He asked you for your help and you refused him. So the typewriter stays here."

Charges

Among my charges, I helped feed the eight priests.
Then Father Pirmin came and changed things. "We
can make our own toast," he said. "We don't have to
come over here. For breakfast, each man can make
his own toast." Then we only served dinner and
supper. We called them "bums" among ourselves.
Father Martin came late one day and called over the
kitchen door: "Can a bum get some dinner?" I had
put a plate aside and went to serve him. He insisted
on eating on the porch. I could have my own dinner
then, so I joined him.

Jumper

I was a hardliner about the habit. The community
sent a seamstress around to the missions and she
asked for mine. "I'm not ready," I said. "I'll wear
my plain wool habit with the modified veil."

"No," she said. "You're going to give me that habit
and I'll make you a jumper." And that's what
she did.

The next day, I went into my first grade classroom
in a jumper with a white blouse. The kids all came
running and put their arms around me and said,
"Oh, Sister!"

But these eighty years of religious life I've worn
my veil.

Mission

"You are not a pretty girl, Georgine," my mother
said, "but you are kind and you love God." At
thirteen, I was on my way to six feet tall. Truth be
told, I wanted to marry, have children and run a
farm. I thought it would be boring to be a nun, too
quiet. But I was sent on mission to Thailand and
got to hear Merton's last talk, hours before his
accident. Afterward, we went to Bangkok. I
climbed up on an elephant's back, feeling the
muscled flesh. He heaved himself up and me, too—
we big, ungainly pair.

Boys

I was prefect to thirty-six wards in our boys' school,
first through eighth grade. They were from broken
homes and a few hoodlums sent to us from the
Cities. I slept in an alcove beside their long
dormitory; a thin wall separated us from the
novitiate. I woke them every morning, got their
faces washed and hair smoothed and to breakfast
on time. They were supposed to demonstrate good
manners, but they were often hungry and stuffed
their mouths with food. After the initial rush, they
settled and were gentlemen the rest of the meal.
They required a lighter hand.

Temper

When I was six a boy kept grinding the pencil sharpener. Sister became so annoyed she unscrewed it from the wall and locked it away. As a teacher, I avoided harsh corrections.

One morning there was such widespread misbehavior I took a moment in the hallway to collect myself. When I returned, thirty kindergarteners sat silent in their seats, looking afraid. Then Jimmy got up from the front row and began to sing. He sang "Hello, Dolly," right up to the part about "we're so glad to have you back where you belong."

How can one stay angry at children?

Reservation Sister: Offerings

We tended our large garden before and after
teaching. The children's parents brought us gifts:
buckets of fish, deer, eggs, chickens. Our hands
always smelled from gutting fish. One night, late,
the doorbell rang; the Indians had brought us a
bear! It required immediate attention. Father
Bernard helped. He held the knife and said: "Well,
there may be more than one way to skin a bear, but
I don't know *any*." He was a good man who had
grown up hunting. The bear was an unpleasant job,
strong smelling and a bit too human-shaped, but
we laughed our way through.

Milk

When we started pasteurizing for the students, I
included the Sisters' supply, too. I sold the milk from
our cows to the plant and got back pasteurized milk
with the same butterfat content. The Sisters wanted
to be sure it was *our* milk. We had a terrible sense of
pride there. I let them think it was ours for two years;
then I let word out. Immediately, the milk didn't
taste as good as it had the day before. It didn't make
financial sense to process our milk separately.
Everyone agreed, but they insisted the milk never
tasted as good.

Charity

The people in Cold Spring were so good to us. We had everything we needed. Mr. Alexander sent his wife to check all the beds. Every bed was bad except for two. Well, there must have been thirty beds. The day JFK was shot, he and the men from the granite company came over and set up all new beds. We also always had beer. The man from the brewery would call and ask, "How is the beer holding out, Sister?" We hated to tell him that all the cases were empty because it seemed they had just been delivered.

Poverty

Once one of the doctors ordered a side of beef. He had it all wrapped up in the freezer for his folks to take back after a visit. Meantime, Sister Cecile gave all of it away to the poor! He came to her red in the face and said, "Didn't you know I bought that for my parents?" She said, "Well, you ought to be grateful. I gave it to the poor on your behalf." Often there were people lining up to get food for free in the back of the kitchen, whatever was left over from the patients' meals.

Uniform

I couldn't wait to begin college with the Sisters and wear the dark blue uniforms with white collars. I liked those because you didn't feel lower class. I've always loved uniforms. We had the habit and then I wore a nurse's uniform, crisp and white. We lived in the large hospital mission on the Mississippi and we were always active. There was ice skating in winter and rowing in summer. Once, in a storm, I jumped from the boat when we were close to shore to help tow in the others. The habit pulled at me, but I was strong.

Flora

I was the first of our Sisters to get a PhD from a secular university. This was the 1920s. None of the Catholic universities offered a doctorate in botany, so I went to the University of Minnesota. I lived in the Josephite convent and took the streetcar. I did the whole degree during summers, teaching biology at our college during the year. I've collected six hundred specimens of the flora of Stearns County, in four collections: flowers of the woods, flowers of the prairies, flowers of the water and swamps and wet places, and flowers of the fields and byways.

Advice

The school chaplain had a suite of rooms and was there to say Mass and give spiritual guidance. Some women hung on his every word, but not me. When I found out Sister Marianne was making his bed every morning, I was appalled. If I had a question, I asked one of the older Sisters. Even in 1946 we thought about women's ordination. I went to Sister Edith and asked her about it. She said, "If you want to be part of the decisions, then you have to be in a position to make them." That was all she said.

Propriety

All three of us teachers in Sauk Centre got a ride to the conference with Father Giles. The bishop said to us, "You daren't travel in a car after dark with a man." We were embarrassed to tell Father Giles we couldn't go back with him.

The next day was Monday, a school day. We traveled to St. Cloud on the St. Joseph local and from there caught the 2 a.m. flyer to Melrose. We napped at the convent a few hours. At dawn we hired a taxi to school—think of the time and expense. All for propriety's sake!

Reservation Sister: Liturgy

There were ten of us to operate the school, clean
the buildings, cook for everyone and do the
laundry. We prayed the Office and went to Mass.
Father Bernard tried to incorporate some Indian
objects into the liturgy: an Indian blanket as an
altar cloth, stoles woven by one of the women, a
reed basket for the Eucharist. He referred to the
Great Spirit in his prayers. But the few reservation
women who came to daily Mass were very
traditional Catholics, wearing lace veils and praying
the rosary while he said Mass. We Sisters, though,
enjoyed what Father Bernard did.

Anointing

I told the chaplain, "Don't be afraid to anoint
people even if they aren't dying." That caused quite
a stir. The sacrament is anointing of the *sick*, not
dying. The doctors complained it scared the
patients. Nurses barred the chaplain's way.

It's the final sacrament; not the end of life. The
English rite says: "If anyone is sick, let them bring
in the priests and let them pray over him, anointing
him with oil." That's from Saint James. When
Father Godfrey educated us on the topic, I sat in
the front pew and nodded often to help my
Sisters along.

Prayer

Before the Council, we had a daily hour of
meditation in chapel between Vespers and Mass.
For many of the Sisters, it was a siesta. One day
elderly Sister Othbert suddenly said in a loud
whisper, "I wish, I wish, I wish I were in heaven!"
Another time, Sister Clarinda woke up and stood,
saying, "Mary, where are we?" Since Vatican II
there is more personal responsibility. We schedule
our own time for *lectio*. I'm sure some don't do it at
all, but many do it faithfully, early in the morning
or after dinner. There's less snoring in
the Oratory.

Community

There were three Sisters who didn't get along and they really wanted to get clear of each other. People were signing up for the new missions that were being started in Iowa, Nebraska and South Dakota. It was all secret, who was signing up for which missions, the selections. All three signed up to go to Iowa. They didn't know; each thought she'd finally be done with the others. In the dining hall the subprioress was reading the names of who would go to Iowa and she read out all three of their names. Well, the dining room just howled.

New York

When I was sent to Columbia University in 1970
to get my doctorate, I just wanted to get it over with
and come home. That doesn't mean I didn't enjoy
New York. About that time, the New York City
Theater (now it's Lincoln Center) had just opened.
The idea was to make theater accessible for
common people. I went to see ballet every Saturday
for two dollars. Ballanchine was all the rage. I saw
musicals, one with Mary Martin. But I never
understood those Sisters who left the convent
and stayed in the city. There was nothing there
but concrete.

Translation

At home I was Greta, but at school they called me Muggs. My religious name is Sister Glenore, which suits me fine.

I went on mission to Taiwan, which was called Formosa then.

When I arrived, the Sisters said they had chosen a Chinese name for me, Gu Ping. I frowned until they explained it means "providence" and "peace."

The next day I went to the town office to register. When the clerk heard my English name, he shook his head.

"She has a Chinese name," the translator said. "It's Gu Ping."

"Much better," he said, and wrote it down.

The Prioress

In 1984, I worked at our Sisters' retirement home.
That year we elected Sister Penny our prioress. So
many of the Sisters were advancing in careers in
secular settings that we struggled to balance
modern life with our vowed life. She was a strong
woman of faith who could help us maintain our
ministries and prayer life; she had been president
of a college. I was sitting with Sister Adelaide,
whose eyesight wasn't good. She asked me, "Who is
that man?" It was Sister Penny, wearing a blazer
and pants, approaching us. "Sister," I said, "That
man is your prioress."

Renewal

One day in 1951, Sister Virginia (the sacristan and
housekeeper) fell against the marble communion
rail in the hospital chapel and it collapsed in a heap
of dust and smoke. We couldn't afford to replace it
and Father Riley asked the diocesan chancellor for
permission to use a small communion table
instead. He said it was on account of infirm and
elderly patients, and he received approval. We
never knew if the bishop himself approved. We
knew Father Riley did it for the nurses. We could
walk right up and receive communion standing. It
was absolutely new. Quite an innovation.

Talk

In 1976, after the national women's ordination
conference, we had a meeting at the college called
"Women in Ministry." Just before we began there
was a commotion—the horses had gotten out and
were running around the parking lot. People were
excited and almost a little scared. We went and
rounded up the horses and it was fine. I was the
emcee, so I began by saying, "I hear that the horses
have broken out of the stable. Could that be a
symbol of what we are doing here today?"
Wouldn't you know that was the headline
the next day.

Sabbath

The life of the farm still tugs at me after all these
years. Although I know it is her only day off, I feel
uneasy when Sister Marybeth does her canning on
Sunday afternoons. Even worse is when I walk past
the full laundry line on my way to church. My
mother would never allow the hanging of laundry
on Sunday, and she had a dozen children to keep
in clean clothes. I don't want to be one of those
cranky, judgmental nuns, so I just let it go.
Every Sunday night I say the rosary, though, a
childhood habit.

Thrift

The hospital opened in 1929, months before the crash. Everything was scarce and we made do. We sharpened hypodermic needles. In the operating room we laid out a new blade for cutting skin and a sharpened blade for organs. We had very few medicines, no antibiotics. Sleeping pills were a last resort. We'd try a rub, then a cup of hot tea, then finally we'd wake the supervisor to administer the sleeping pill. In our kitchen was a picture of St. Thérèse of Lisieux. The frame was used X-ray film and it hung by a piece of old IV tubing.

Vocation

I thought I'd like to be a Dominican because they always looked so scholarly. Then I thought: "That's no way to join." So I prayed, "Lord, you'll have to show me."

After a year out, in 1925, I figured it was time. I didn't join for the glamour, actually.

These days, I'm so tired of hearing young women say: "I'm going to try the life. It's so beautiful and peaceful." Stuff like that. You don't try it out; you go because it's what God wants. How many marriages would have been avoided if they asked, "Is this what God wants?"

Statio[1]

Sister Petronilla and Sister Cosma

Sister Bibiana and Sister Venantia

Sister Narcissa and Sister Willibald

Sister Maximine and Sister Mechtildis

Sister Vincentia and Sister Frowina

Sister Clyde and Sister Herberta

Sister Philothea and Sister Emmerama

Sister Borgia and Sister Stanislas

Sister Mavilla and Sister Theodosia

Sister Chrysostom and Sister Noemi

Sister Ludwina and Sister Severa

Sister Patrick Joseph and Sister Benora

Sister Angelinda and Sister Engelbert

Sister Meinulpha and Sister Domitilla

Sister Theophane and Sister Cleopha

Sister Hilberta and Sister Humbeline

Sister Bonaventura and Sister Ehrentrudis

Sister Ulrich and Sister Rodelia

---

[1] For definition of *Statio*, see note on page 58.

Sister Ildephonse and Sister Paschaline

Sister Othmar and Sister Emerentia

Sister Heliodora and Sister Servilla

Sister Boniface and Sister Bernard

Sister Tilberta and Sister Leonilla

Sister Roger and Sister Harvette

Sister Leocadia and Sister Ventilla

Sister Placida and Sister Hubertine

Sister Radegundis and Sister Cunigundis

Sister Alacoque and Sister DeBritto

Sister Elfleda and Sister Lamberta

Sister Martinette and Sister Ignatius

Sister Bertilia and Sister Gabriel

Sister Rosaire and Sister Loyola

Sister Basil and Sister Juetta

Sister Kenneth and Sister Ermenilda

Sister Kevin and Sister Ludovica

Sister Veneranda and Sister John

Sister Eulalia and Sister Borromeo

Sister Dympna and Sister Bozena

Sister Aaronette and Sister Maxentia

Sister Constette and Sister Jerome

Sister Dignata and Sister Irmalin

Sister Conchessa and Sister Thecla

Sister Doralia and Sister Paul

Sister Anrico and Sister Etienne

Sister Gregor and Sister Roderick

Sister Redempta and Sister Trinita

Sister Goretti and Sister Marvin

Sister Sebastine and Sister Elmer

Sister Donalda and Sister Phillipa

Sister Sylvan and Sister Providentia

And 1,152 more, in pairs, process, bow, and take
their places.

Notes and Dedications:

The raw material for these stories began with books that collect interviews with Roman Catholic nuns in the United States and conversations. But very early on I focused in on the riches of the oral histories of the Sisters of the Order of Saint Benedict in St. Joseph, Minnesota.

I was the communications director for this Benedictine community from 2008-2011. I got to know a number of the Sisters, witness their lives and hear their stories. I am grateful for their friendship. I live on 80 acres that was once the Sisters' hog farm, a mile from the monastery. It has been called at times St. Isidore's Farm and Grace Acres, a name we often use for it.

The Sisters of the Order of Saint Benedict founded their community in 1857 in Central Minnesota. At their peak in the 1950s, they had 1,254 members. They founded seven other monastic communities in the United States, missions in the United States and foreign countries, and numerous hospitals and schools. Many Sisters came from the German Catholic farm towns near the monastery. They founded the College of Saint Benedict in 1913.

Because all of these pieces are transformed to varying degrees from the original and many of them are composites or products of my imagination from a small seed in the material, I have decided to provide dedications for them rather than sorting through the biographical origins. In some cases, where the connection to a particular Sister is more important or preserved, I've noted that. One should not assume that the Sisters in the dedications are the direct source of the material in the stories; that is not always the case.

I am deeply indebted to the work of those Sisters who collected the oral histories, particularly to Sister Etienne Flaherty, and to Sister Clare Shadeg, who assembled detailed topical indexes of the material contained in them, as well as to Sister Renee Rau and the rest of the staff of the monastery archives. I know what a gift it is to be trusted with these stories and I hope the Sisters find something here of value.

The stories here are loosely organized around the lifespan of the Sisters and the timespan of the histories I worked with, primarily covering the period of the 1920s-1980s. There are stories here from the three areas of life emphasized in the Benedictine community I know: prayer, community and work.

Habits: Dedicated to Sister Kara Hennes, who first told me about the sewing machines.

Life's Liturgy: Dedicated to the Weber and Arceneau sisters and the many vocations from St. Martin, Minnesota.

Music: This story is adapted from the oral history of Sister Cecile Gertken (1902-2001). Sister Cecile was an advocate for the use of Gregorian chant in the liturgy. With Br. Bartholemew Sayles of Saint John's Abbey, she wrote English texts for the chant and was a significant figure in music and liturgy. The talented Gertken family is known for its contribution to the two monasteries. Of nine children in the family, three brothers were priests at the abbey (the fourth died while a deacon preparing for ordination) and four of the five girls entered the monastery. The fifth daughter never married and was the town postmistress.

Vice: This story is adapted from the oral history of that faithful rebel, Sister Jeremy Hall (1918-2008).

Formation: Dedicated to Sister Owen Lindblad, who continued to go sledding until she was eighty years old.

Names: Sister Margretta is Sister Margretta Nathe (1913-2007) and this is her story, though many speak of going to the cemetery in search of a name.

Particular Friendships: Many of the Sisters talk about the prohibition against "particular friendships." And many of the Sisters now enjoy the bonds of genuine, close friendships that seem especially important in age and in a large community. The inspiration for this particular story is owed to the oral history of Sister Jeremy Hall.

Hitching: For my mother-in-law Betty Mandell Heymans, who came to the College of Saint Benedict a dairy farmer's daughter from Faribault and left a teacher.

Typhoid: The accounts of the typhoid outbreak came from several sources, including S. Suzanne Helmin, S. Glenore Riedner and S. Emeric Weber (1914-2003), who contracted the illness. The account of the confession is solely hers. There was also good information on the typhoid and the relative lack of infection and illness despite primitive food storage methods by S. Jameen Mape (1906-1995).

Mary: This story belongs to Sister Lawrence Kiffmeyer (1904-1993) and her sister, Sister Omer Kiffmeyer, both nurses, who kept their names even when others went back to their baptismal names.

Crows: For Sister Katherine Kraft, who laughs generously, who walks my neighborhood now without a chaperone and who is loved by every child she meets.

Turkey Girl: For Sister Carolinda Medernach (1912-2011).

Cellarer: The cellarer has a particular role in a Benedictine monastery, which is to distribute goods. The position held by S. Jameen Mape was purchaser and dietitian, but she cared for the food and was as judicious as any cellarer. The story "Milk" is also adapted from her oral history.

Mission: For Sister Glenore Riedner (1902-2007) who lived to 105, heard Thomas Merton and rode an elephant. As a child she hunted muskrats with her brothers on their farm in Bird Island, Minn. "Translation" is also her story.

Gym: For Sister Jameen Mape.

Gifts: For Sister Victorine Houde, pharmacist (1913-2010).

Charges: For all the Sisters who have worked to care for others behind the scenes.

Jumper: For Sister Suzanne Helmin (1912-2011).

Boys: For Henry Borgerding (1889-1989), who was one of those charges, and Sister Emeric Weber, both of whom told stories about the boys' school, which the Sisters ran at the convent from 1898-1938.

Temper: For Sister Suzanne Helmin, who loved to tell the "Hello, Dolly" story, and whose students still visited when they were in their 70s and she was 99.

Reservation Sister: Offerings: The two stories set on the reservation are dedicated to the many Sisters who worked on the remote, frontier Ojibwe missions of Red Lake and White Earth. It was without a doubt a mixed experience for both the Sisters and the Native Americans, who found ways to nourish each other richly from their traditions and their gifts.

Charity: For the people of St. Cloud, St. Joseph, Cold Spring, and all the little towns who helped take care of the Sisters. The Sisters earned very little and sometimes donated their salaries back to the hospital or church where they served.

Poverty: For the seeds of this story, "Anointing," "Thrift" and "Renewal," I am indebted to Father Patrick Riley (1918-2010) who was chaplain at St. Cloud Hospital from 1951-1968 and left a wonderful, full account of life with the Sisters during this time of change.

Uniform: For Sister Victorine Houde, who provided the inspiration.

Flora: Based on the life of Sister Remberta Westkaemper, who taught at the College of Saint Benedict from 1919-1973.

Advice: For Sister Ruth Nierengarten, dear friend.

Propriety: This story is based on an account in the oral history of Sister Alana Fleishhacker (1893-1993).

Reservation Sister: Liturgy: (see "Offerings" above)

Prayer: For Sister Marlene Meierhofer, whose lamp I saw winter mornings when I arrived at work in the dark as she did her daily *lectio*, and all the Sisters who continue to pray faithfully daily.

Community: For all those Sisters who learn again and again that you don't ever get to choose your family, and the prioresses who have kept them in relationship.

New York: For the Sisters whose obedience took them to places they didn't want to go and who made the very best of it.

The Prioress: For Sister Barbara Kort, who is a treasure trove of stories.

Talk: For those Sisters whose full vocations were not able to be realized and yet who remained faithful to the Church and their vows.

Sabbath: For Sister Gen Maiers, who taught me so much during my three years about fundraising and mission and leadership and what it means to be a Benedictine Sister, and whose mother had seventeen children and never did laundry on the Sabbath.

Thrift: For the Sisters who sacrificed so much, not just the hospital staff but every Sister of Saint Benedict's Monastery, to pay off the debt incurred building St. Cloud Hospital in 1928.

Vocation: For the women currently in discernment and all those who choose to become Sisters not for "the glamour" but because God calls.

*Statio: *Statio* is a Latin word that describes a form of procession whereby the monks or Sisters enter in two rows. When they reach the altar they turn, bow to each other, then take their places on the two sides of the choir or assembly. The Sisters continue to process in *statio* to this day, but it is very difficult to imagine the days when there were 1,200 or more in the community.

Acknowledgments

"Habits" and "Home Visit" first appeared on the website 100 Word Story magazine: www.100wordstory.org

Many of these pieces were first posted on the author's page at http://cowbird.com/author/susan-sink

Susan Sink blogs at http://susansink.wordpress.com

Cover design and illustration by Steve Heymans: http://stevehdesign.com